ARCTIC OCEAN

ASIA

OPE

MEDITERRANEAN
SEA

China

India

SOUTHEAST
ASIA

AFRICA

PACIFIC OCEAN

Pacific
Islands

New
Guinea

INDIAN OCEAN

AUSTRALIA

To my first loves, the Martin twins.
— M. L.

To my mother, Mildred Long, who taught me to read,
one of life's greatest gifts.
— T. L.

To my sons, Matthew and John,
who continue to be the source of my greatest joy and pride.
— S. L.

We wish to thank the Wildest Club in Town (the Phoenix Zoo Support
Group), Frank Murray (spectacled bear enthusiast) for providing
us with the most recent information on this elusive bear, and Martha
Carlisle Tacha (wildlife biologist) for her advice and support.

Also thanks to Laura Jane Coats for her excellent
suggestions in designing this book.

Text ©1995 by Matthew Long and Thomas Long. Illustrations ©1995 by Sylvia Long.
All rights reserved. The illustrations in this book were rendered in pen and ink and watercolor.
Typeset in Rotis Serif. Printed in Hong Kong. Book design by Laura Jane Coats.
Library of Congress Cataloging-in-Publication Data
Long, Matthew, 1975-   . Any bear can wear glasses/
by Matthew Long and Thomas Long; illustrated by Sylvia Long.
p.   cm.   ISBN 0-8118-0809-2
1. Animals-Juvenile literature. 2. Endangered species-Juvenile literature.
[1. Endangered species. 2. Rare animals.] I. Long, Thomas, 1946-   . II. Long, Sylvia, ill. III. Title.
QL49.L85   1995   591-dc20   94-46642   CIP   AC
Distributed in Canada by Raincoast Books, 8680 Cambie Street, Vancouver, British Columbia V6P 6M9
10   9   8   7   6   5   4   3   2   1
Chronicle Books
275 Fifth Street, San Francisco, California 94103

Any Bear Can Wear Glasses
The Spectacled Bear & Other Curious Creatures

by Matthew Long & Thomas Long · illustrated by Sylvia Long

Chronicle Books · San Francisco

Any bear can wear glasses. . . .

Sloth Bear

Sun Bear

Polar Bear

Asian Black Bear

but there's only one spectacled bear.

Of the eight *species* of bears, only one, the spectacled bear, has fur markings that make it look as if it's wearing glasses. Once found throughout North and South America, spectacled bears now live in the wild only in or near the rain forests of South America's Andes mountains. Spectacled bears are excellent climbers and can travel quickly through the leafy canopy of the rain forest. They are most active at night, when they spend most of their time hunting for food. Spectacled bears primarily eat tropical plants and fruits. They will occasionally eat small *mammals* and birds as well. Spectacled bears usually spend their days resting in nests either hidden on the ground or high up in the trees.

The male spectacled bear lives alone, except during mating season. Cubs, usually born one or two at a time, are raised by their mother, who builds a nest under tree roots to shelter them until they're about one month old and their eyes finally open. The cubs make a humming noise when they're nursing and call to their mothers by making a trilling sound when they are separated from her. When very small, the cubs may ride on their mother's back, snuggled into her fur. They stay with her for six to eight months before going off on their own.

There are only a few thousand spectacled bears alive today. Due to the destruction of their rain forest *habitat*, especially by slash and burn farming, they have become an *endangered species*.

Any lizard can get dressed up...

Chameleon

Gila
Monster

Monitor
Lizard

Short-Horned
Lizard

but there's only one frilled lizard.

The frilled lizard gets its name from its unusual frill, a skin fold around its neck that opens up like an umbrella. The lizard raises its frill to make itself look bigger and more powerful, usually when it feels threatened. The frilled lizard grows to about three feet in length and its opened frill can be about a foot across. When the frilled lizard feels threatened, in addition to opening its frill, it stands on its hind legs, hisses, and whips its tail back and forth. It's all just a big show, though. If this display fails to frighten the *predator,* the frilled lizard will quickly run away on its hind legs, using its big tail for balance.

The frilled lizard can be found in Australia and New Guinea. It lives much of its life in trees, seldom coming to the ground except to eat — especially after a rain storm when its favorite foods, insects and spiders, are more active. It will also sometimes eat small *mammals*. When the female frilled lizard's eggs hatch, her offspring immediately begin searching for food and taking care of themselves.

The frilled lizard is a *threatened species* because humans are damaging its *habitat.*

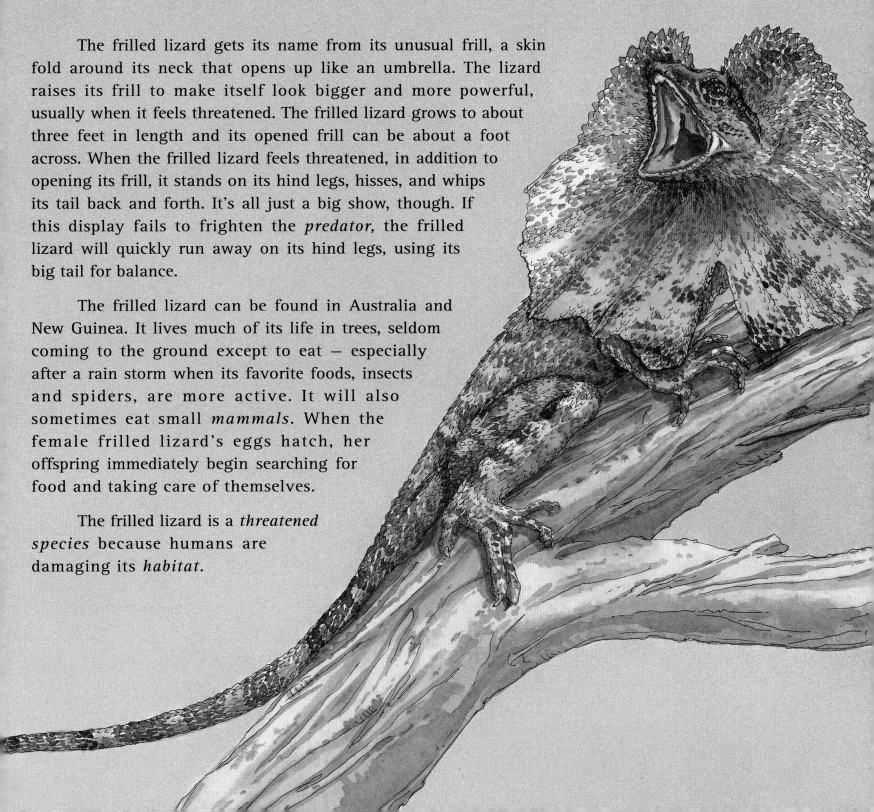

Any cat can wear jewelry...

Tiger

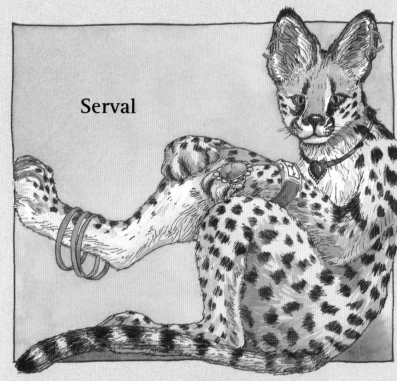

Serval

Ocelot

Cougar

but there's only one ringtail cat.

The ringtail cat looks and behaves like a cat, especially when it licks its paws and cleans its face after eating, but it is really more closely related to bears and raccoons. There are two *species* of ringtail cat. One is found in Central America and is almost *extinct.* The other lives in North America, from the deserts of the Southwest to the coastal forests of the Pacific Northwest.

The ringtail cat is a *nocturnal* hunter, and is primarily *carnivorous.* It stands on its hind legs to hunt for lizards, mice, and other small *mammals.* Ringtail cats also eat cactus fruits, acorns, and berries. They live in dens, usually in natural holes in decaying trees or openings in rocky cliffs. When natural dens aren't available, ringtail cats will move into man-made structures, especially abandoned houses and barns. The ringtail cat is about thirty inches long including its tail, but weighs only about two pounds. Like a skunk, the ringtail cat can produce a terrible smell when it's frightened. Also, it can curl its tail up over its body to make it seem larger to a *predator,* such as an owl or bobcat.

One to four babies are born in each *litter.* They're blind and helpless at birth, with short, coiled tails. After about a month, their eyes open. In two months they're ready to leave the nest and go hunting with their mother. The beautiful rings develop within four months, and at this time they are ready to go off on their own.

The North American ringtail cat is not an *endangered species,* but it is *threatened* by logging and human development of its remaining *habitat.*

Any swan can play an instrument...

Black Swan

Whooper Swan

Mute Swan

Tundra Swan

but there's only one trumpeter swan.

The black-beaked trumpeter swan is named for its distinctive call — which sounds like a trumpet. Two hundred years ago, the trumpeter swan was found in great numbers throughout central and western North America. But since then, it has been hunted by humans for its meat and feathers, nearly to *extinction*. Protective laws and *conservation* work have helped restore its numbers, but it remains an *endangered species*.

The trumpeter swan is an *herbivore*, and eats water plants and grasses. Trumpeter swans mate for life, and once each year the pair builds a nest on the water's edge in which it *incubates* its eggs and raises its *brood*. Each clutch, or group of eggs, usually contains four to six eggs. It takes about five weeks for the eggs to hatch. The female swan *incubates* the eggs while the male protects their *territory*.

Baby swans are called cygnets, and when they hatch from the eggs they are covered with fuzzy down. After the first or second day, the cygnets can leave the nest and look for food, but they are carefully protected by their parents. To make it easier for the babies to get their food, the mother will often use her feet to stir up the plants underwater. This is called "puddling." The cygnets stay with their parents for about a year before going off on their own.

When fully mature, the trumpeter swan is one of the heaviest of all flying birds, weighing as much as thirty-five pounds. It's so heavy that, like an airplane, it needs to get a running start to take off into the air.

Any monkey can wear a hat...

Baboon

Emperor
Tamarin

Mandrill

Vervet
Monkey

but there's only one capped langur.

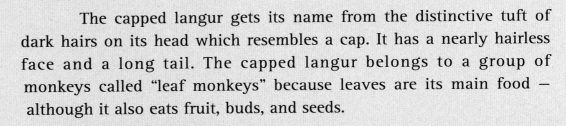

The capped langur gets its name from the distinctive tuft of dark hairs on its head which resembles a cap. It has a nearly hairless face and a long tail. The capped langur belongs to a group of monkeys called "leaf monkeys" because leaves are its main food — although it also eats fruit, buds, and seeds.

The capped langur lives in the forests of India and Southeast Asia. It seldom comes down from the trees except to get water, or if the distance to the next tree is too far to jump.

Capped langurs live in groups of twenty or more, usually with only one *dominant* male. Different groups of langurs will often interact without establishing *territories*. Capped langurs spend about half their time sitting quietly in treetops digesting their leafy meals. Because it can look as if they are praying at these times, some local people believe capped langurs to be sacred.

The female capped langur usually has just one baby each year, which is completely helpless at birth and is carefully nursed and cared for by its mother. Its yellowish-brown color turns grayer as it grows older. After about a month, the baby begins to play games of chase, wrestling, and tree-leaping with the other baby langurs in its group. The young monkeys are not ready to go off on their own until they are three or four years old.

Because of the continued destruction of the rain forests of Southeast Asia the capped langur has become an *endangered species*.

Any crab can make music...

Ghost Crab

Blue Crab

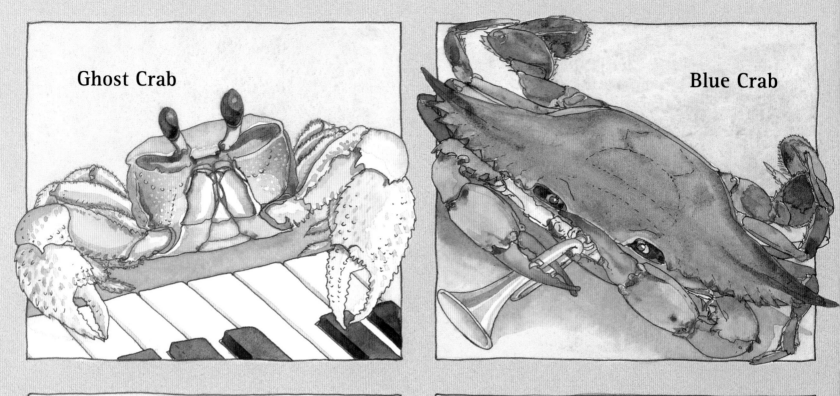

Hermit Crab

Rock Crab

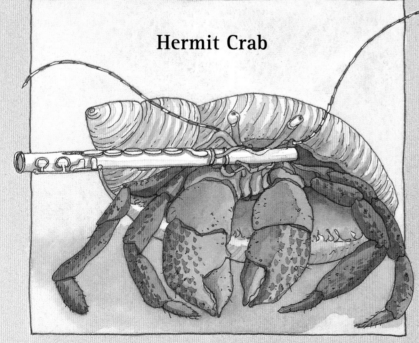

but there's only one fiddler crab.

Male fiddler crabs have one front claw, or pincer, that is much larger than the other. It is so big that it can be half the total body weight of the crab. Many *species* of fiddler crabs hold their large claw up in the air and move it back and forth, as if playing a fiddle or violin — which is how they got their name. The males use the large claw to drive away intruders from their *territory* and to attract female fiddler crabs during their courtship dance. Each of the different fiddler crab *species* has its own special dance pattern. For instance, some stand on tiptoe and wave their pincers in circles above their heads. When a female is attracted by the male's courtship dance, she follows him into his burrow beneath the sand. Her fertilized eggs later hatch into tiny *larvae*. These gradually become mature crabs by shedding the hard shell covering each time the crab's body outgrows it. The outer layer of skin then hardens to become the crab's new larger shell. These body changes are called moltings.

The female fiddler crabs have only small pincers. Both males and females use their small pincers to lift food such as plankton and *algae* to their mouths. The many other legs of the crab are used to sort the food and throw away uneaten sand and waste, which is deposited on the surface of the sand in little round pellets. When fully grown, the fiddler crab is one or two inches wide.

There are many varieties of fiddler crabs living in marine areas throughout the world. Many are *threatened* by *pollution* of their *habitats*.

Any rabbit can wear shoes...

European
Rabbit

Eastern
Cottontail

Brush
Rabbit

White-tailed
Jack Rabbit

but there's only one snowshoe hare.

The snowshoe hare is named for its large back feet which grow stiff hairs in the winter. These large feet help it to walk on the snow without sinking in. The snowshoe hare's fur is brown to gray in summer months and white in the winter. These color changes serve as *camouflage* to make it harder for *predators* to see the hares.

Snowshoe hares are found throughout the forests of North America. In summer, they live above ground in dens formed in evergreens or willows and eat grass, weeds, buds and bark. In winter, they live in hollows in the snow or earth formed by packing the area down with their feet, and they eat branches, twigs, and stems.

Female snowshoe hares, called does, have two to six *litters* each year with two to four babies in each. The babies are called leverets. Hares are born with fur and open eyes, unlike rabbits who are blind and without fur at birth. The leverets depend on their mother's milk for the first week of life, but begin eating grass in the second week. After about a month, they are strong enough to be on their own. Leverets can run pretty well even a few hours after birth, and by the time they are fully grown, snowshoe hares can run forty miles per hour!

Any fox can travel...

Red Fox

Kit Fox

Gray Fox

Arctic Fox

but there's only one flying fox.

Flying foxes aren't foxes at all; they're really fruit bats. They get their name from their fox-like faces and big eyes, which help them gather light when feeding at night. Flying foxes live in the tropical forests of Africa, Asia, and the Pacific Islands.

Many people are afraid of bats, but bats are very important to the balance of life on Earth. Flying foxes help spread the pollen and seeds of tropical plants. Some trees, like the eucalyptus in Australia, depend on flying foxes for pollination to survive.

Flying foxes sleep hanging upside down in trees or caves, often in large groups or colonies. They are *mammals*, and their single babies are born blind and without fur. When they are first born, they must be protected under their mother's wings and are nursed for four to six months. Baby flying foxes grow hair after only a few days and can fly on their own by the time they are about three months old. When fully grown, some *species* of flying foxes are very large, with wingspans of over five feet.

Flying foxes are decreasing in number and *threatened* in all the areas where they are found. They are hunted for food, and their forest *habitat* is being destroyed. Several *species* have already become *extinct*.

Any cat can fish...

Jaguar

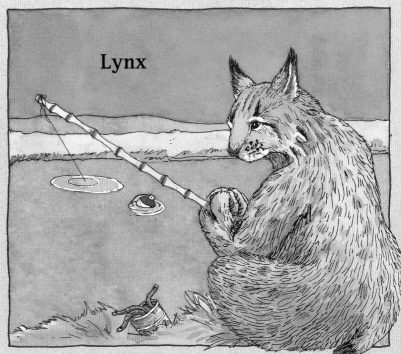

Lynx

Cheetah

Lion

but there's only one fishing cat.

Fishing cats really do fish! They lie on the banks of streams or wade out into the water to catch fish with their claws or teeth. The fishing cat also likes to eat small *mammals, crustaceans,* frogs, birds, and insects. Fishing cats are among the larger cats living in India, Southeast Asia, and China. They weigh about thirty pounds, and have short legs, a short tail, a chunky body, and close-set eyes.

Fishing cats live alone most of their lives, but live in pairs during mating season and when raising young kittens. Two or three kittens are born in each *litter.* They weigh only about six ounces each and can fit in the palm of a human hand. They are nursed by their mother for about four months. Little else is known about the fishing cat's life in the wild, except that leopards, pythons, and crocodiles are their natural *predators.*

Water *pollution* and the destruction of their forest *habitat* have made the fishing cat an *endangered species.*

Any iguana can wear a uniform...

Rhinoceros
Iguana

Land
Iguana

Fijian
Banded Iguana

Green
Iguana

but there's only one marine iguana.

The marine iguana got its name because it is the only lizard that lives in and around the ocean. It is found only in the Galápagos Islands, off the west coast of South America. The marine iguana eats the *algae* and seaweed that grow on the rocks along the shoreline, both above and below the water. Other iguanas only eat plants on land.

Marine iguanas grow up to five feet in length and have sharp claws to help them walk on the slippery rocks. They also have a broad tail, like an oar, which helps them to be excellent swimmers. They wave their tails from side to side, like a snake, to move through the water. Marine iguanas are dark gray, but some develop bright red spots when trying to attract a mate.

The female iguanas dig tunnels in which they bury their eggs. As soon as the eggs hatch, the baby iguanas begin to search for food. When the marine iguanas are not busy swimming and feeding, they rest in the sun on the rocks. The females and young often cluster together in big colonies, but the males stake out and defend small territories. If one male invades another's *territory*, the two iguanas will butt heads together until one finally backs away in defeat.

Since humans discovered the Galápagos Islands, many animals living there, including the marine iguana, have become *endangered* because of hunting, *habitat destruction*, and *pollution*.

Any duck can wear a disguise...

Ruddy Duck

Harlequin Duck

Mallard

Spectacled Eider

but there's only one masked duck.

The masked duck is named for the black mask on the face of the males. This small duck is found in the tropics, ranging from the Caribbean to the Mexican Gulf Coast, and south to Peru and Argentina.

The masked duck has a long stiff tail which it uses to swim underwater. It's a very good swimmer and can swim both forwards and backwards. It can stay under water for thirty seconds or more at a time, feeding on underwater plants, insects, and *crustaceans*.

The masked duck uses two unusual tricks to escape its *predators*. If it wants to hide, instead of diving below the water, it can quietly sink straight down without making a splash. If it wants to flee, it can dive below the water in one spot, swim ahead a few feet, and come out of the water flying!

Masked ducks form temporary pairs to mate and build nests, but the *brood* of four to six ducklings is cared for only by the female. They nest in marshes or in areas covered with water plants, like lilies, for added protection.

The masked duck is a *threatened species* because of *habitat* destruction.

Glossary

Algae
Small, usually microscopic plant life, which is a major source of food for many animals.

Brood
A group of young animals cared for by its mother.

Camouflage
A natural-looking disguise which helps an animal blend into its environment.

Carnivore
An animal which eats other animals.

Conservation
The protection of natural resources through careful planning and management.

Crustaceans
Animals that live in water and have a hard protective shell, two pair of antennae, and gills.

Dominant
The animal in a group that is the leader or that controls the others.

Endangered Species
A species in danger of becoming extinct. Scientists label a species endangered if they feel it will disappear completely unless action is taken to save it. Most of the animals in this book are endangered or *threatened* species. In fact, some experts predict that within fifty years, one fourth of all the Earth's species could be extinct.

Extinction
The complete elimination of a *species*. It is thought that 50 to 150 species are becoming extinct every day as a result of destruction of the world's rain forests, where more than half of the Earth's species live.

Habitat
An animal or plant's native environment.

Habitat Destruction
The loss of natural environments. Sometimes this can be due to natural forces, such as a volcanic eruption or an earthquake. But natural habitats are also destroyed by human actions such as logging, pollution, and expansion.

Herbivore
An animal which eats plants.

Incubation
The way animals keep eggs warm, usually by sitting on them.

Larvae
The newly hatched stage of certain animals which go through several changes before developing into adults.

Litter
A group of offspring from a single birth.

Mammal
Any back-boned, warm-blooded, and usually hairy animal which is born alive and relies on nursing milk from its mother to live and grow.

Nocturnal
Active at night.

Pollution
The release of harmful substances into the environment.

Predator
An animal which hunts other animals.

Species
A group of animals or plants which can only reproduce successfully within their group. For example, all human beings are of the same species. There may be 5 to 30 million species living on Earth, but only about 1.4 million of these have been identified and named.

Territory
An area of *habitat* claimed by an animal or group. Often the territory will be guarded and defended against intruders.

Threatened Species
A *species* which is likely to become endangered soon. There are more than 600 species in the United States alone which are listed as threatened or *endangered*, and many more are threatened worldwide.

ARCTIC OCEAN

Greenland

Pacific
Northwest

NORTH
AMERICA

Southwest

Mexican
Gulf
Coast

GULF OF
MEXICO

ATLANTIC OCEAN

CARIBBEAN
SEA

CENTRAL
AMERICA

PACIFIC OCEAN

Galápagos
Islands

Peru

SOUTH
AMERICA

Andes Mountains

Polynesia

Argentina

WHAT'S YOUR NAME?

From Ariel to Zoe

photographs by Marilyn Sanders

text by Eve Sanders

Holiday House/New York

PRONUNCIATION GUIDE

Ariel: AR-ee-el

Blakely: BLAYK-lee

Charlotte: SHAR-lot

Diego: Dee-AY-goh

Eva: EE-va

Fredron: FRED-RON

Gabe: GAYB

Hana: HAH-nah

Ian: EE-an

Jesse: JESS-ee

Kossi: KOH-see

Lily: LIL-ee

Meave: MAYV

Nate: NAYT

Orit: OR-eet

Preston: PRESS-ton

Quincey: KWIN-see

Rebecca: Reh-BEK-kah

Shandiin: SHAHN-deen

Tess: TESS

Urai: YUR-eye

Veerta: VEER-tah

Whitney: WIT-nee

Xavier: SAH-vee-er

Yuki: YOO-kee

Zoe: ZOH-ee

With appreciation to Wally McGalliard, master printer, who made the exhibition prints of the photographs in this book.

Text copyright © 1995 by Eve Sanders
Photographs copyright © 1995 by Marilyn Sanders
ALL RIGHTS RESERVED
Printed in the United States of America
FIRST EDITION

Library of Congress Cataloging-in-Publication Data
Sanders, Eve.
What's your name? : from Ariel to Zoe / Eve Sanders ; photographs
by Marilyn Sanders. — 1st ed.
p.   cm.
ISBN 0-8234-1209-1
1. Names, Personal—Juvenile literature.   I. Sanders, Marilyn.
II. Title.
CS2377.S26   1995   95-9771   CIP   AC
929.4—dc20

For Henriette, with our love

Even before a child is born, parents think about choosing the right name. How does it sound? Will it bring the child luck?

A name can be long or short, new or old. It can be borrowed, passed down, or made up from a special word.

Children have names from all different languages: Japanese, Latin, Yoruban, Hebrew. Languages from everywhere in the world: Spanish, Hopi, Russian, Farsi. Hindi, Arabic, Chinese, Swedish. What language is your name from?

Sometimes people make jokes about your name. Or they say it wrong.

You can make up a nickname. Spell your name backward and create a new name. Friends can think of secret names and not tell anyone else.

> Wherever it comes from,
> Whatever it means,
> Your name is yours,
> To write in big letters or small,
> To whisper or shout,
> To say: here I am. . .

ARIEL. I can write my name in Hebrew or just English. Ariel means "lion" in Hebrew. At the park, I climb trees and act wild. I like being animals with claws — lions, tigers, bears, alligators, crocodiles. I like how lions roar.

BLAKELY. I looked up my name in a book. Blakely means "from the black meadow." It makes me think of rain and storms. I play volleyball with my mom. My dad said I should learn basketball, too, because I'm going to be tall. So I joined a basketball team called "The Rockets."

CHARLOTTE. There were a hundred Charlottes in my dad's family before me. Two were great-great-great aunts who lived in Vermont. My dad built me this tree house, and I helped with the sanding. I got a diary for my birthday. I only write in it when I'm up here.

DIEGO. My father is a painter. I was named after the Mexican painter Diego Rivera. And after San Diego, California, where we used to live. It sounds different, but "James" is English for "Diego." My parents bring me to the beach to play. Later I draw pictures with lots of blue for the sea.

EVA. My name is for remembering my great-grandma. Her name was Eva, too. In Hebrew, Eva means "life." Every Sunday, my dad and I go someplace: the museum, the park, the beach. I feel happy when I can run with my dad. I drive fast in my wheelchair. I zoom around and explore.

FREDRON. Fredron is my father's name, too. I want to be an artist because my grandfather is an artist. I learned to draw from comic books. Now my grandfather is teaching me technique. He showed me how the light changes everything. My eyes are green in the sunshine.

GABE. There is an angel in the Bible named Gabriel. But I'm named after my mom's best friend. He's Big Gabe; I'm just Gabe. My mom started the garden. It has over a hundred flowers. The orange flowers smell sweet. White flowers smell like hand lotion.

HANA. I'm six, but I'm small for my age. My name is Hana. My parents decided to call me that name before I was born. They said it means "graceful." My frog's name is Jessica. I say things she doesn't understand. She only understands frog language. Look! She feels comfortable in my hand now.

IAN. I'm named after John, my father's friend. But our family is Scots. The Scots name for "John" is "Ian." So my parents named me Ian instead of John. My friends call me "E." Once, I was on a boat, and a blue shark came up out of nowhere. Today, all I saw was a cloud of seagulls.

JESSE. My grandfather died just before I was born, and I'm named Jesse because of him. In the Bible, Jesse is the father of King David. I listen to country music with my mother and rock music with my father. At my aunt's wedding, I played the piano when no one was looking. I have to wait for my hands to grow bigger, and then I can take lessons.

KOSSI. Kossi, my middle name, is from West Africa. It means "a boy born on Sunday."
My first name is Solomon. When my mother held me right after I was born, I didn't cry. I
opened my eyes wide and looked straight at her. She said I looked so wise, she decided to
call me Solomon after the king in the Bible. I love, love to swim, but this water's too cold.

LILY. I like my name because there are flowers called lily. My mom got me a bulb, so I could grow lilies in the backyard. I can say my name in Latin, too: Lilium. Sophie is the neighbor's dog. She comes over and falls asleep in front of our house. Once she let me ride on her back.

MEAVE. In Irish stories, Meave is Queen of the Fairies. Some people call her "Mab." My brothers and sisters have Irish names, too. I visit my mother's bakery after school. It smells like bread and cinnamon. If my mom lets me, I always eat the same thing—a chocolate eclair.

NATE. No one calls my by my real name: Nathaniel William. Nathaniel means "given by God." I like to be called Nate. Sandy is my rabbit. Sandy could be a girl's name or a boy's name, but Sandy is a girl rabbit. I had to tell her a secret. The secret was, I love you. And I heard her say: munch, munch.

ORIT. My family is from Ethiopia. My grandfather said that in Harar, the language we spoke in Ethiopia, Orit means "kind and generous." My friend showed me how to blow bubbles. You take the gum, you put it in your mouth, you chew it, you blow the gum. Then you get a bubble.

PRESTON. Preston is a place in England. Preston Sturges was a movie director, and I'm named after him. I like tae kwon do, books about Egypt, and the TV show with Toby the Tram Engine. My name is OK, but I'd rather be called Toby. Can I be called Toby from now on?

QUINCEY. My mother always says my first name and middle name together: Quincey Miguel. She had a grandfather, two uncles, and a cousin named Quincey. Miguel is Spanish, to remember Paraguay, the country where I was born. It's far away on the map. I'm going to be a superhero when I grow up and fly there.

REBECCA. My mom wanted to be called Rebecca when she was little, after a girl in a book: *Rebecca of Sunnybrook Farm*. That's why she gave me that name. But I like Grace, my middle name, better. It sounds pretty. I keep a piece of string in my pocket so I can play cat's cradle wherever I go.

SHANDIIN. I dance when my father is drumming on his drums, and I make up songs. I sing about things that happened to me. I sing about people I know. I sing out my name — Shandiin! In Navajo, my name means "sunshine."

TESS. I'm named after my mother's favorite poet: Tess Gallagher. I like ballet the best. You get to dance in the mirror. You get to run and jump and pirouette. You get to wear a leotard, ballet shoes, and a tutu.

URAI. No one else in the world has my name. My mother invented it. She says I danced before I walked. Maybe I'll be a dancer in a company one day. Then I could go to all the places on the globe and listen to the music of all those places.

VEERTA. My mother made up my name from a Hindi word. The word "veer" means "bravery" in Hindi. I think my name is like a gift from my mother. Sometimes I remember my name and I feel brave.

WHITNEY. I'm named after a mountain: Mount Whitney in California. My twin sister is my best friend. We do art projects together and draw pictures. We draw our dog and cat and parakeets. Or we draw each other.

XAVIER. My name is Xavier and I'm strong. I have a Spanish name because I'm Spanish and my dad is Spanish. And my *abuela*, my grandmother, she is Spanish. *X* marks the spot where the treasure is buried. I look for treasure at the beach. And sea urchins. They can sting you. Watch out for crabs. They tickle.

YUKI. When we moved here, the first three things I learned to say were: Hi, OK, and My name is Yuki. Starting school was scary because I didn't know any English. In Japan, shy is nice. Here it isn't such a good thing. I had to change myself. I learned to play handball, and I made new friends. In Japanese, Yuki means "courageous."

ZOE. Sometimes my parents call me "Zo" instead of "Zo-ee." They said my name is Greek and means "life." I don't like to lose when I play cards with my grandmother. I hide the bad cards under the sofa. My grandmother said, What should I do with you? I said, Wind me up and let me go.

Alphabet of names,
from all kinds of places,
who do you remember,
whose names and whose faces?

Ariel,
Blakely, Charlotte, Diego,
Eva, Fredron, Gabe;
Hana, Ian, Jesse,
Kossi, Lily,
And Meave;
Nate and Orit,
Preston and Quincey,
Rebecca and Shandiin;
Then, Tess and Urai,
Veerta and Whitney,
Xavier, Yuki, and Zoe!

No two sound alike,
no two are the same,
one is still missing,
What's *your* name?